LOOK AND FIND

Walt Disney's

GOOFY

AND FRIENDS

HUNT FOR THE GREAT GOOFINI

Illustrated by Jaime Diaz Studios

Illustration script development by Christina Wilsdon
Lettering by Kelly Hume

Published by
Louis Weber, C.E.O.
Publications International, Ltd.
7373 North Cicero Avenue
Lincolnwood, Illinois 60646

ISBN 0-7853-0105-4

PUBLICATIONS INTERNATIONAL, LTD.

A note that says *Help!* is all that remains of the Great Goofini! Mickey and his friends have no choice but to look for the missing magician. They'll need his magic wand, though. Can you help them find it?

Can you find these other magic things, too?

The magic wand

The ace of hearts

Paper flowers

This rabbit

A magic mirror

A crystal ball

A saw

TICKET SELLER

With a wave of Goofini's wand, Mickey and his pals are hot on the trail of their missing friend. First stop: Madame Mousaka's fortune-telling caravan.

Is the Great Goofini here? You bet! But his friends can't find him. Can you? Can you also find these spirits that Madame Mousaka has summoned?

The Great Goofini

Ma Barker

King Toot

Short John Silver

Libby the Kid

Erik the Green

In a blinding flash of light, Goofini finds himself lost in an ancient Egyptian pyramid. "Abracadabra!" says Mickey, and the gang find themselves in the pyramid, too!

Can you find the Great Goofini? Can you decide what he has lost? Look for these treasures in the mummy's tomb, too.

The Great Goofini

A giant pearl

A golden horse

A golden cat

A basket of rubies

A giant diamond

EGYPTIAN RECORDS

THE LATEST IN WRAP MUSIC

AKHENATON + NEFERTITI

EMERGENCY FIRST AID

SEWING KIT

101 RIDDLES OF THE SPHINX

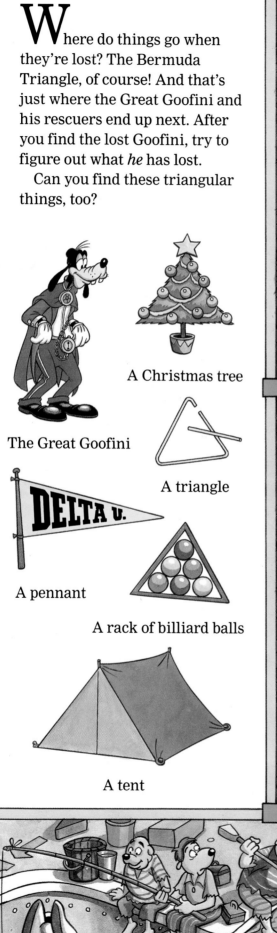

Where do things go when they're lost? The Bermuda Triangle, of course! And that's just where the Great Goofini and his rescuers end up next. After you find the lost Goofini, try to figure out what *he* has lost.

Can you find these triangular things, too?

The Great Goofini

A Christmas tree

A triangle

A pennant

A rack of billiard balls

A tent

Crazy ol' Professor Frankenpoodle was expecting quite a different outcome to his latest experiment when Goofini burst onto the scene—with Mickey and the others right behind!

Can you find Goofini? Can you figure out what he's missing now? Look for the Professor's silly inventions, too.

Turtle trailer home

Goofini

Polka-dotted zebra

Snake skates

Instant sweater

Kangaroo with a zipper

Ain't nobody here but us 'gators and zombies—'cept fer this here feller who done stopped by fer a bite! Too bad he don't know he *is* the bite!

Poor Goofini is really swamped this time! After you decide what he's missing, see if you can find these hungry swamp critters.

This alligator

This rat

This snapper

This vulture

This spider

This snake

This panther

Doesn't it drive you *batty* when unexpected guests arrive? Not the Count and Countess Von Quack. They have plenty of extra caskets…er…*beds* for overnight guests.

While Goofini wonders about his weird host and hostess, try to figure out what he has lost so far. Then look for these fellow guests.

Baron Overbite

Fiona Fang

Drake-ula

Madame Midnight

Dawn Newday   Colonel Corpuscle

Run, Goofini, run! And *don't* stop to smell the flowers! Can you find the Great Goofini in this jungle full of creepers and crawlers? Can you tell what he's lost this time?

Once you've found Goofini, look for these plants that would love to have someone drop in!

Goofini

Venus's-mousetrap

Jolly Roger

Pluto's-dogcatcher

Deadly lampshade

Deadly nightshade

Weeping widow

DO NOT
EXIT

A-maze-ingly, Goofini has found his way back to the County Fair from which he suddenly disappeared during his magic show!

Mickey can see his long-lost pal, but he can't figure out how to reach him! Can you?

Find Goofini and the rest of the gang. Then look for the solution to this fun-house maze!

Goofini

Goofini's rabbit

Mickey

Minnie

Pluto

Donald